Acting Edition

I0741562

Nan and the Lower Body

by Jessica Dickey

ISBN 978-0-573-71138-1

www.concordtheatricals.com
www.concordtheatricals.co.uk

MUSIC AND THIRD-PARTY MATERIALS USE NOTE

IMPORTANT BILLING AND CREDIT REQUIREMENTS

NAN AND THE LOWER BODY was originally commissioned by the Manhattan Theatre Club. The artistic director was Lynne Meadow, the executive producer was Barry Grove, with funds provided by the Alfred P. Sloan Foundation. *NAN AND THE LOWER BODY* was originally produced by TheatreWorks, Silicon Valley, Palo Alto, CA., as part of their New Works Festival on July 13th 2022. The artistic director was Tim Bond, the managing director was Phil Santora. The performance was directed by Giovanna Sardelli, with scenic design by Nina Ball, costume design by Cathleen Edwards, lighting design by Pamila Z. Gray, sound design by Jane Shaw, and wig design by Heather Sterling. The cast was as follows:

DR. GEORGE PAPANICOLAOU. . . . . Christopher Daftsios

NAN DAY . . . . Elissa Beth Stebbins

MACHE PAPANICOLAOU . . . . Lisa Ramirez

TED DAY . . . . Jeffrey Brian Adams

CHARACTERS

DR. GEORGE PAPANICOLAOU – (aka **DR. PAP**) – Mid-60s, short, Greek, handsome in an odd way, in a way that grows on you. A truly unique scientific mind. Mischievous, good-humored, perceptive, charismatic, subversive, more tenacious than most.

NAN DAY – 20s/30s, tall, New England, pretty in a quiet way, in a way that grows on you. Extremely bright, very reserved and buttoned-up, but more emotional than she lets on. Not good at small talk or meaningless jokes. Trying to hide symptoms of a serious health crisis.

MACHE PAPANICOLAOU – Wife of George. Late 50s to early 60s, short, even stout, not attractive but not unappealing, built with an unusual amount of discipline, blunt, has worked long and hard with her husband, but is recently losing her place at his side.

TED DAY – Husband of Nan. 20s/30s. Liberal New England minister, incredibly earnest and socially forward-thinking, perhaps easily shocked, his ideals make him miss the subtler things sometimes. He became a minister to hug the world. A positive extrovert.

Nan also plays The Playwright.
Mache also plays Older Nan.
Ted also plays Older Ted.

Please cast as diversely as possible.

SETTING

A lab at Cornell, the Papanicolaous' living room,
and other locations.

TIME

1952.

AUTHOR'S NOTE

The smell of Jergens lotion. Her yellow and white shawl. Cranberry juice mixed with orange juice. The vroom vroom of her motorized wheelchair. The gaspy wheeze of her laugh. Her trembly signature.

My maternal grandmother Nan lived with my family from the time I was five until her death, nineteen years later. Due to multiple sclerosis (MS), she was in a wheelchair, paralyzed from the waist down. I resemble her – strawberry hair and cheeks, a crooked front tooth. She and my grandfather lived in the room off our kitchen, and that meant every morning the downstairs smelled of powder and urine, a combination I came to associate with decay. I knew my grandparents were going to die, so I kept them at a distance, sometimes tiptoeing past their room so they wouldn't hear me. We ate at the same table every night, but I failed to really know them.

For example, many years after her death, I learned that Nan worked as a cytologist, pioneering the identification of cervical cancer. My Uncle Mark believed her boss had been none other than Dr. George Papanicolaou, the creator of the Pap smear. We know for sure that Nan was a good cytologist, when her multiple sclerosis made it impossible to commute, the hospital installed a lab in her home so she could continue working. My uncle remembered coming from school and finding her bent over the microscope, crying, because the cells before her were from a young mother who had stage four. At a time when most women did not work, let alone have a career, Nan was carving an unusual legacy in her field against the ticking clock of a debilitating disease.

I don't know if Nan really worked for Dr. Papanicolaou. I wrote this play as a way to dream that possibility into existence. To step inside that dream and sit with her again. But better this time. More deeply this time. To take her hand and ask questions. To share my life with her in a way that I couldn't bear back then. To tell her that I'm sorry. And that I see her now.

Jessica Dickey

For Nan

One

(Cornell University. 1952.)

(DR. GEORGE PAPANICOLAOU – *60s, Greek, handsome in an odd way, in a way that grows on you – is there before his audience.)*

DR. PAP. I love the sound of pencils.

Bss bss bss bss bss

Just now I was closing my eyes, listening to your pencils go

bss bss bss

and it was like a magic spell was gathering its strength.

(He likes this idea.)

Or even better –

Like some secret part of ourselves is whispering to the secret selves around us,

"Bss bss bss – Hey! Hey there!

I'm here, you're here – let's

do something,

eh?"

(He is very charming in his style, his manner – masculine, commanding, clearly brilliant, but also mischievous and winning. He continues –)

"Bss bss bss."

– this is the sound of our secret selves conspiring, you got that, right? –

"Bss bss bss – Let's *do something*!

What should we do?

I know! –:

Let's talk about something most people never talk about.

Let's see a world most people never see.

Let's go *inside the female body*!"

I'm not drunk I swear.

Well maybe I'm a little drunk.

haha no I'm not.

Let's go inside the female body!

– bss bss bss! –

Let's prostrate ourselves before the mystery of the reproductive galaxy!

And let's ARM ourselves against anything

that might *harm* that strange and precious space.

Boy, are you sorry you signed up for this.

You came here to learn about the Pap smear! –

The new technique for identifying cancers in the female reproductive system! Far less invasive than the current biopsy procedure – and FAR more *effective*... Just a simple sample of the vaginal fluid and everything can be seen...

> *(And just like that, he has effortlessly entered his spiel.)*

According to the most recent analysis, released just last year in 1951, cancer of the lower body and reproductive system is currently *the number one killer of women.* Think about that. Women, mothers, sisters, are dying every day. But with the vaginal smear, early detection is possible, this is a fact. Today I –

(*He stops.*)

Wait a minute – where's my new assistant? What's her name again? Nan Day. Where is Nan?! Is she late? SHE'S FIRED! No that's a joke. *(Very sad.)* Oh Nan is late! Well, we need to forgive her. She departed very early this morning to begin her training with me. I know, you're thinking "Poor her" – well you're right! – but don't worry – if her application is any indication it is ME you should be worried about because I can tell you, she is quite formidable.

She was the only woman to apply. Imagine that! A position for women's health and only men applied! The female sex is not exactly prized in the medical sciences, are they? Shame on us.

Ah, which reminds me – yes, let's just get this out of the way –:

Vagina.

Vagina.

(*Making them get used to the word.*)

Vagina vagina vaginal fluid.

Vagina.

Okay? Good? Okay. I've done this many times you know, and I've learned it's good to just – get that over with. Now –

(**NAN** *suddenly bursts through an upstage door. She is attractive in a quiet way, in a way that grows on you. She is mortified to find an audience staring at her.*)

NAN. Oh God!

DR. PAP. Ah! You must be Nan!

> *(Perhaps from the shock, her leg gives out and she falls. He immediately goes to help her up. Intending to lighten the mood –)*

Are you alright?

NAN. Yes, thank you.

DR. PAP. Well – now I can say you fell for me. That's just a joke. We were just talking about you! Well, vaginas actually, but also you.

> *(She looks at him; there'll be no more humor of that sort. He gently bows a little, extends his hand, his demeanor suddenly that of a great scientific mind and leader.)*

I am Dr. George Papanicolaou. You can call me Dr. Pap. I am immensely pleased to make your acquaintance.

NAN. Dr. Papanicolaou, forgive the, we had train trouble, and. Anyway. Not exactly the first impression I prefer to make.

DR. PAP. Good thing it wasn't then. Your first impression was your unusually moving cover letter, and your high marks and qualifications. Do you remember the part of your application where you described the flowers? What was the example you used?

NAN. Phlox.

DR. PAP. Yes, Phlox! Tell them.

> *(She looks at the audience.)*

NAN. Uh – people often confuse Phlox with Dame's Rocket. They look almost identical, both are a showy, erect, branching plant, about four feet high, same colors. But if you look carefully, Dame's Rocket has four petals in its flower, whereas Phlox has five. Which you can remember by the fact that Phlox has five letters – p-h-l-o-x.

DR. PAP. Isn't that wonderful? I loved that part of your application. I couldn't think of a better perspective with which to approach this work. *(To continue his lecture.)* Now if you don't mind...

NAN. *(Relieved.)* Yes of course.

> *(She exits off the stage toward the back of the house.)*

DR. PAP. *(Returning to the audience.)* You didn't think I'd forgotten about you...? No such luck! I was just giving you time to recover from the word VAGINA.

Now:

(With great aplomb.) How To Spot Squamous Cell Carcinoma With The Vaginal Smear Technique!

> *(Blackout.)*

Two

> (**DR. PAP** *trains* **NAN** *in the lab. Beakers, materials, microscopes, in the corner an examination table with stirrups. He clips right along. She is nervous, but focused.*)

DR. PAP. Now once material has been accumulated from both the outside and the inside of the cervix, we *smear* the material – hence the name – onto a slide, and voila. You are ready for the stains. Come.

> (*He leads her to a series of little containers of different colored fluids.*)

First we must prepare the cells for the staining sequence. We rinse the slide in different graduated alcohols like so – 95 percent alcohol, 70 percent alcohol. Then we dip it in water to rehydrate the cells before the hematoxilyn, that's the purple reddish fluid there. Ready?

NAN. Oh. Yes.

> (*She takes the slide and dips in each fluid.*)

DR. PAP. Good – yes – and now put it in the hematoxilyn. Good, and now we set the timer for five minutes and we wait.

> (*He sets the timer.*)

So. What about your husband?

NAN. What about him?

DR. PAP. Well, let's start with his name.

NAN. Theodore. But he goes by Ted.

DR. PAP. And he just took a new job as well, correct?

NAN. At a charity organization, but that's just until he gets a parish.

DR. PAP. A parish. So he is a...?

NAN. A minister, yes.

DR. PAP. And how is that for you?

NAN. How is what for me?

DR. PAP. Theodore-who-goes-by-Ted being a minister.

NAN. Oh. Uh. *(She checks the timer. Not even close.)* It's fine. It's uh, well, it's a *calling*. So.

DR. PAP. Being the spouse of a minster is not so easy, no?

NAN. I'm not sure it's much harder than being the spouse of a scientist.

DR. PAP. *(He chuckles.)* Touché. So you understand my line of inquiry.

NAN. I'm not sure I do actually.

> *(There's something in his familiarity, and probably her nerves, that makes her prickly, and she's the kind of person who prickles when she's prickly.)*

DR. PAP. Does he support your work, Ted née Theodore?

NAN. Meaning...

DR. PAP. Does he expect you to pop out a baby as soon as he feels settled in his post despite your promising new position as the assistant of Dr. George Papanicolaou, the creator of a technique that will revolutionize women's health around the world...?

> *(He smiles. She doesn't.)*

NAN. No.

DR. PAP. No what?

NAN. No I don't believe "Ted née Theodore" thinks me the sort of person to "pop out" anything, let alone a baby, and I am quite certain he respects my considerable mind and what I choose to *do* with it, including my current post.

> *(Quick beat.)*

DR. PAP. Good.

NAN. What is good, Dr. Papanicolaou?

DR. PAP. Your anger. I see you have goals for your life.

NAN. Oh, we're talking about my *goals*? I thought we were talking about my husband. If we're talking about my goals, then yes I want a family. And I want to be an exceptional cytologist. I would like, very much, to do good work. Work that affects lives for the better... I'm not particularly talented. I seem to only be good at patience. And detail. And being myself. But that'll have to do.

> *(Did she just blow that? Then the timer dings.)*

DR. PAP. Now we use an acid alcohol to remove any excess hematoxilyn from the cytoplasm. Then a submersion in tap water substitute, go ahead. Then we stain with OG-6, named for its orange color, you see – go ahead – And then we set the timer for two minutes.

> *(He sets the timer for two minutes.)*

Your family must be very excited for you.

> *(It's like a game – strict instruction, then over personal questions. He enjoys it. She doesn't.)*

NAN. To be married?

DR. PAP. Of course not, everyone gets married, it's not an accomplishment. I mean to be working on the Pap smear.

NAN. No one's really heard of the Pap smear.

DR. PAP. Not yet, but they *will*. The whole world will have heard of the Pap smear by the time I'm through. And then your job will be easier.

NAN. My job?

DR. PAP. Someone has to carry on this work when I'm a hunk of dead meat. It should be a woman. Cervical cancer is a crisis in the medical community; women are dying and we don't know what to do about it. And yet they scorn me! "Oh Dr. Pap and his fixation with female anatomy!" Malakismeni. (*Greek for "fucking idiots."*)

But the fact is – the world is very very *funny* about women.

Just like the world is very funny about ethnicity. You might be thinking what does he know? – He's white – but before I am white I am *Greek*. And believe me, that's a distinction for some people. Here at Cornell, the Pathology Department wouldn't hire me, did you know that? But you're thinking, he created the Pap smear! No matter; I was a dirty Greek. So here we are: In the *Anatomy* Department.

(*A dark, conspiratorial twinkle.*)

But you know what? I say these people are smart.

NAN. Smart?

DR. PAP. The status quo know a threat when they see one. They took one look at my work and they *knew*. It will be the same with women like you, Nan. They will sense that something is on the verge of breaking, and that they are on the losing side. So they will fight you, just as they fight me. And they are quite right to fear you, just as the Pathology Department was smart to block me. For I'm going to *annihilate them all.*

(*The timer dings.*)

(*Immediately returning to a chipper tone.*) This next step is quite quick, we just rehydrate the cells. Like so.

(*They put the slide in water.*)

And now we wait. Just one minute.

(*Timer. Back to the game.*)

So you want children.

NAN. I do.

DR. PAP. Mache and I agreed very early there would be no children. I wanted to make a serious contribution to science, you see. Have you considered that?

NAN. Dr. Papanicolaou –

DR. PAP. Dr. Pap.

NAN. – Dr. Pap –

DR. PAP. Everyone calls me Dr. Pap. I like it. It's like (*À la a hip person.*) – Hey! Dr. Pap! (*Back to himself.*) It's good.

NAN. Dr. Pap. Perhaps we could save the personal questions for another occasion.

DR. PAP. Ah.

NAN. If you wouldn't mind.

(*He regards her.*)

DR. PAP. You're quite strict.

NAN. I'm quite –?

DR. PAP. Strict, you're quite strict. Was your father strict?

NAN. *(Sore spot.)* Yes.

DR. PAP. It's good to have a strict father. To develop an early sense of *earning your worth*. This idea that we are enough as we are, just for *being*, this will be the demise of society. Only important work makes a life worth living.

NAN. Not everyone feels that way.

DR. PAP. Of course not. And not everyone is *capable* of important work. But for those who are... Nothing less is worthwhile. And a strict father helps.

> *(The timer dings.)*

(The conspiratorial twinkle returning.) I'll tell you a secret – when I am talking to someone who doesn't know much about my work – I am very fond of using the word "vagina" as much as possible.

NAN. People know the word vagina.

DR. PAP. Of course they *know* it, but they are not *used* to it. So they *squirm*. I have a – how do you say – a *sixth sense* for such a person – it's really very wonderful, you should try it.

Now. We are ready to look at it under the microscope. Go ahead and put the stains on the counter, I'll set us up over here.

> *(The slide is ready.* **NAN** *gets up to put the containers of stains on the other side of the room and buckles just slightly as she rises.)*

Oop-pah. Alright?

NAN. Yes thank you.

> *(She continues cautiously with the containers and sets them down. This is not lost on him.)*

DR. PAP. Now attach the slide on the stage there, that's right, and then use the knobs there to assess the slide in a zigzag formation. You read the booklet I sent you on various signs of abnormal squamous cells.

NAN. Yes.

DR. PAP. Tell me the three types of normal squamous cells.

NAN. The squamous superficial cells, mature with plenty of estrogen, making the nucleus a tiny little dot.

DR. PAP. Yes.

NAN. The intermediate cells, with a slightly larger nucleus –

DR. PAP. – yes –

NAN. And the parabasal cell, where the nucleus-cytoplasmic ratio is most narrow. Very common in menopausal women. These are the cells that are most likely to be confused with cancer.

DR. PAP. Correct, and how will you differentiate between a normal parabasal cell and a cancerous one?

NAN. The normal parabasal cell has a smooth nucleus edge, whereas a cancerous one will have uneven edges, like a raisin.

DR. PAP. Correct. Do you like raisins?

NAN. *(What?)* No. Well. I like them on their own, not *in things*.

DR. PAP. In things?

NAN. Yes. Like muffins.

DR. PAP. You don't like them in muffins?

NAN. No.

DR. PAP. Cake?

NAN. No.

DR. PAP. Pudding? Surely you like raisins in your pudding...

NAN. No.

DR. PAP. Bread?

NAN. No.

DR. PAP. I love raisins in bread! I love everything in bread. The raisins, the nuts, fruit, the chocolate, put all of it in! Okay. I have a meeting with the Dean. *(Mocking academia.)* Ooooh. *(Back to business.)* Organize these slides, we'll review them when I return.

NAN. Okay.

> *(He leaves. He reappears, popping his head around the door.)*

DR. PAP. What about cereal?

NAN. – What?

DR. PAP. Cereal?? Raisins in your cereal??

> *(She stares at him for a moment. Then concedes –)*

NAN. I do like raisins in my cereal.

DR. PAP. *(Raising his fist in a kind of athletic victory.)* The raisin gets a vote! Wonderful!

> *(And with that he is gone. She sits there in momentary disbelief, then chuckles, charmed in spite of herself. She gets up to place a tray of slides on the shelf and suddenly her legs buckle and she falls, crashing slides all around her.)*

> *(**MACHE** enters.)*

MACHE. This is not good.

NAN. Oh god, I'm sorry.

MACHE. Don't apologize to me, you're the one covered in slides of vaginal fluid. Let me help you.

> (**MACHE** *goes to* **NAN.** *To her great relief, feeling in her legs has restored and* **NAN** *is able to get up. They clean up the slides.*)

NAN. I'm so embarrassed.

MACHE. *(With a shrug.)* Once I farted in front of the Dean.

> (**MACHE** *is about sixty, short, even stout, not attractive but not unappealing, built of an unusual amount of discipline, has a blunt, somewhat off-putting style.*)

I'm Mache. Dr. Pap's wife.

NAN. I'm Nan.

MACHE. Yes. Nan.

NAN. He's not here, he had a meeting with the Dean.

MACHE. I know. I wanted to meet you.

NAN. *(Huh.)* That's very kind.

> (*An awkward pause. Then –*)

Well, I guess I should get back to –

MACHE. I brought a tray of slides. Dr. Pap forgot them.

NAN. Oh?

MACHE. Yes. He walked right out the door without them.

NAN. They were at home?

MACHE. Hm?

NAN. The slides, they were at home?

MACHE. Yes.

NAN. *(Huh.)* If you want to wait, he said he wouldn't be long.

MACHE. No no. I want *you* to give them to him.

NAN. *(Huh.)* Me?

MACHE. Yes.

NAN. Alright. I will.

> (**MACHE** *just stands there, though the obvious interaction that's appropriate has ended.*)

MACHE. When I was your age, I was in despair about my life. I didn't feel like other girls. I didn't look like them, I didn't behave like them. For all outward evidence I was on the path to being a spinster. Or the wife of an ugly butcher. No offense if your father is a butcher.

NAN. My father is not a butcher.

MACHE. Really? Your father could've been a butcher.

NAN. Why do you say that?

MACHE. You seem like someone who has seen the red flesh of a large mammal hanging from a hook.

NAN. ...

MACHE. Don't worry, I too am such a woman.

NAN. Was your father a butcher?

MACHE. My father was in the military. So – yes. What does your father do?

NAN. He worked in a shoe factory.

MACHE. He's retired now?

NAN. He's dead. He died when I was eighteen.

MACHE. How did he die?

NAN. The factory caught fire. Everyone was trapped inside. I was hired by the local hospital to examine the bodies and I found him. I put a tag on his foot that said his name.

MACHE. Was that difficult?

NAN. On the contrary. Seeing my father's body helped me... It made me who I am.

MACHE. You see? – The red flesh of a large mammal hanging from a hook.

> (*A beat. It's like* **MACHE** *is trying to take the measure of this young woman before her.*)

What kind of name is it? *Nan.*

NAN. A nickname.

MACHE. A nickname for what?

NAN. (*Realizing it doesn't make sense.*) Grace.

MACHE. Grace?

NAN. Yes.

MACHE. Your name is Grace?

NAN. Yes.

MACHE. Grace to *Nan*? It is not an improvement.

NAN. Oh, I don't know. Names have a funny way of revealing who we really are.

MACHE. Is Grace not who you really are?

NAN. Grace seems to make so many promises... I like Nan. It's plainer. What kind of name is Mache?

MACHE. It's Greek. From Andromache.

NAN. And what does it mean?

MACHE. Battle.

NAN. (*Not wanting to say the obvious.*) There you have it.

MACHE. For a while they called me Mary. The people here. Well, the wives of the people here. I tried it out for a while, then went back to Mache. You should come to dinner.

NAN. Oh that's –

MACHE. Next Sunday six p.m.

NAN. I'm sorry, on Sunday my husband Ted has services all morning and then meetings through the evening.

MACHE. Next Saturday?

NAN. Saturday we said we would dine with the Cavenaughs.

MACHE. The Cavenaughs?

NAN. Yes, do you know them?

> *(It's like watching two blunt knives try to make an incision reserved for a finer blade – these two straightforward women, different as they are, negotiating the social field.)*

MACHE. The Cavenaughs have never invited *us* to dinner.

NAN. Oh... –? –

MACHE. Mrs. Cavenaugh's knees rub together when she walks.

NAN. Beg your pardon?

MACHE. Mrs. Cavenaugh's knees rub together when she walks. If a person has knees that rub together, their illiotibial band has to compensate. Their *foundation* is not sound. The following Wednesday?

NAN. Sorry? Oh – the following Wednesday would be fine.

MACHE. It's settled.

> *(She gathers her things. Turns back –)*

You'll tell George I stopped by.

NAN. Yes.

MACHE. *(Very pointed.)* And you'll be sure to give him the slides.

NAN. *(Gets that it's pointed, but no idea why.)* I will.

MACHE. Goodnight.

> *(She leaves.* **NAN** *stands holding the slides, deep in thought. She suddenly feels off and decides to sit down at the microscope, carefully setting the slides down next to her. She looks at her leg, rubs it a little, very worried. Then suddenly she punches her own leg.)*

NAN. *(Ferocious.)* Stop it!

> *(She punches her leg again, more ferocious, frustrated.)*

Stop it!

> *(Then* **DR. PAP** *enters.)*

DR. PAP. Here we are!

NAN. *(Recovering quickly.)* Hello!

DR. PAP. Are you unwell?

NAN. No, no, I'm fine. Although – I'm afraid I – I dropped these slides earlier. Your wife arrived just in time to help me, otherwise I'd probably still be collecting them from the floor.

DR. PAP. Mache? Mache was here?

NAN. Yes. She brought those slides.

> *(He realizes which slides* **MACHE** *brought.)*

DR. PAP. Ah.

NAN. She said you had forgotten them at home.

DR. PAP. Did she now.

NAN. Shall I just put them over here with the others?

>(**DR. PAP** *lets out a heavy sigh, perturbed.*)

DR. PAP. *(Clearly agitated.)* Yes, just... No no, leave them there. I'll... –

NAN. Is something wrong?

>*(Beat.)*

DR. PAP. No, no, it's not... She knows very well I didn't forget them, she...

>*(Another sigh.)*

NAN. Is everything alright?

DR. PAP. Perhaps we'll end a little early today. You must be exhausted from your trip. And of course your wedding! You're probably still catching up. But come in early tomorrow if you can.

NAN. Very well.

>*(She gets up, hesitates, uneasy.)*

It looks like Ted and I will be joining you for dinner in a few weeks.

DR. PAP. *(Preoccupied with the slides from* **MACHE**.*)* Wonderful.

>*(She carefully collects her coat and purse. When she is at the door –)*

NAN. Goodnight.

DR. PAP. *(Means it.)* Nan? It was a good first day.

>*(She leaves. He takes the slides* **MACHE** *brought and holds them for a moment. He might even touch them tenderly, sadly. Then he puts them in the trash.)*

>*(Blackout.)*

Three

(The next morning. **TED** *and* **NAN** *enter the lab. She moves effortlessly around the space, hanging up her coat, etc., no trace of the previous spell. In this process she notices the slides that* **MACHE** *brought are in the trash. She sets them on the table.)*

NAN. Ted, I already said yes!

TED. But surely you can tell them you hadn't checked with me, I have this church event, blah blah. They'll understand.

NAN. Why don't *you* go back to your church event and explain to them that you hadn't checked with me, that I have this dinner with my boss, "blah blah."

TED. Nan.

NAN. What? You need to support me.

TED. We ended our honeymoon early, that's support, isn't it?

NAN. We'll have other vacations.

TED. It wasn't a vacation, it was a honeymoon.

NAN. I realize.

TED. I was mooning with my honey.

NAN. Ted, I'm serious. God knows how many dinners I'm going to sit through for you over the next fifty years, listening to old men with giant cactuses of white nose hair, extol the Apostles' creed. You can make this one dinner happen for me.

TED. You do realize I'm eventually going to *be* one of those old men with giant cactuses of white nose hair.

NAN. All the more reason.

(He puts his arms around her. She lets him.)

TED. Our kids running around our hips. Little Bippy and Boppy.

NAN. *(Laughing, a familiar game.)* Ted.

TED. What? Little Ink and Dink.

NAN. We are not naming them that.

TED. Well what then?

NAN. Mmmm. I like Sara.

TED. Sara.

NAN. Yes. And maybe – Mark.

TED. Sara and Mark. They'll be preacher kids – which is kind of a thing, you know –

NAN. Oh yes, I know – they'll probably be anxious! –

TED. Very anxious!

NAN. But they'll do good things in the world. And maybe one day *they'll* have children. Who'll do good things in the world. Who knows.

TED. *(Likes it very much.)* Sara and Mark and Ted and Nan.

NAN. Maybe.

(He regards the lab.)

TED. *(Excited and interested.)* So this is where the magic happens, huh?

NAN. Well, not much magic yet. I still have a lot to learn.

TED. So, what's he like?

NAN. Who?

TED. Dr. Papanicolaou. You were so tired last night I didn't really get to hear anything.

NAN. Uh – he's uh – he's interesting.

TED. Uh oh.

NAN. No uh oh, there's no uh oh.

TED. You only say *interesting* when you really don't want to say the word you mean.

NAN. That's not – well, that is true. I don't know, he's very. Um. Pushy. I guess.

TED. Pushy.

NAN. Yes.

TED. Pushy like how.

NAN. I don't know.

TED. Well, like, what did he push?

NAN. Nothing really, it's just his – style or something. Not entirely without charm, mind you, just – pushy.

TED. I guess that makes sense. Here's this man, forcing the world to take women's health seriously. I guess he's gotta be pushy.

> *(He sees the examination table, with its stirrups, in the corner of the room.)*

(The stirrups.) What are these for?

NAN. That's where the woman puts her feet.

TED. *(Yikes.)* What??

NAN. The woman puts her feet in here and slides down –

TED. Slides down?? Hanfry.

> *(Hanfry is like his own little cuss word substitute. Like "eee gads." He's a nerd. A wonderful preacher nerd.)*

NAN. *(Pushing his naïveté.)* And then the doctor uses instruments like this.

> *(She holds up to the speculum.)*

TED. *(Innocent horror.)* What is that??

NAN. It's a speculum. To open the woman so the doctor can see the cervix.

TED. *(Playing it up.)* Holy God.

NAN. Alright.

> *(He makes the speculum like a crab.)*

TED. *(A crab voice.)* "I'm going to eat you!"

NAN. Ted!

TED. *(Laughing.)* You have to admit, it's pretty shocking stuff if you're not used to it.

NAN. It's science.

TED. *(Taking her in his arms.)* It is. And you're a part of it.

NAN. Don't suck up.

TED. *(A laugh.)* I'm not sucking up!

NAN. Yes you are. I haven't forgiven you.

TED. For what?

NAN. For the DINNER.

TED. Ah the dinner.

NAN. Yes the dinner.

TED. I love it when you're cross. You get that wrinkle on your forehead.

NAN. You'd better not give me too many reasons to wrinkle my forehead, you're the one who has to look at it every day for the rest of our lives.

TED. *(Tenderly.)* I think I'll manage. Oh hey! – I scheduled the interview for the parish in Lunenburg.

> *(This is his dream job.)*

NAN. You did?! *(Fingers crossed.)* Oh Ted!

TED. I know, I'm so nervous.

NAN. They are going to love you.

TED. God I hope so! – And get this – *(Proudly.)* they asked me if my wife would be joining me for the interview, and I said, "No sir, my wife is a *cytologist*."

NAN. *(Pleased.)* What'd he say?

TED. Gesundheit.

NAN. Ha!

TED. And then I made him listen to me crow about how you found this opportunity posted at the hospital in Wenham, how you knew the Pap smear was a big deal because as opposed to your male counterparts you actually *read* medical publications... How you nailed the application and got the job. How you're going to be able to get hired at any hospital in the country once you're through.

NAN. That's the idea...

> *(She chuckles humbly but also loves it. He smiles at her.)*

TED. You're right.

NAN. About what?

TED. The dinner. You're right. I'll tell the church I have to reschedule.

NAN. *(Touched.)* Really?

TED. This dinner is important for you, and I will be there.

NAN. Thank you, Ted.

TED. *(Getting a little sexy.)* Oh you can thank me.

NAN. Oh can I?

TED. Oh yes.

> *(They cuddle for a moment –)*

NAN. Okay now get out. I have work to do.

TED. Yes, Mrs. Day. *(Her new name! A kiss.)* Mrs. Day!
(Whirling her around – she laughs.) Mrs. Day, Mrs. Day!

> *(Another kiss.* **DR. PAP** *arrives.)*

DR. PAP. Good morning.

NAN. Oh!

TED. Oh hanfry! So sorry!

NAN. I'm so –!

DR. PAP. Don't worry, don't worry...

NAN. *(Incredibly flustered.)* We were just – ? – errrrr –

TED. I was just about to – haaaaaaahhh –

NAN. He was just on his – yes –

DR. PAP. Okay, stop. I am the lead scientist in women's
reproductive health. Calm down.

TED. Ha!

NAN. Right. Yes. Thank you.

DR. PAP. No thanking, no need for thanking, continue if
you wish –

NAN. No no we're done.

TED. Yes I was just leaving.

DR. PAP. Are you not going to introduce me?

NAN. Oh my goodness, my manners, yes, Ted, this is Dr. Papanicolaou –

DR. PAP. Dr. Pap

NAN. Dr. Pap. Dr. Pap, this is my husband Ted.

DR. PAP. Ted-née-Theodore!

TED. That's me! It's wonderful to meet you, sir.

    (They shake.)

DR. PAP. *(Sizing him up.)* And you, and you.

TED. I so admire what you've accomplished. Nan is very excited, thank you for everything.

DR. PAP. Yes of course. And you, you must be very proud of her, yes?

TED. Oh yes, sir, very proud indeed.

(Winking at her with his little inside joke.) Not to be *pushy*, but I think she's going to do a great job.

    *(**DR. PAP** tracks that he's on the outside of something.)*

DR. PAP. I hope so. What we're doing is very important, you know?

TED. Absolutely.

DR. PAP. The health of the *vagina* is not enough of a priority all over the world.

TED. *(Vagina.)* Indeed.

DR. PAP. *(Vagina.)* The *vaginas* of the world have to be safeguarded by science and exceptional medical care, you see. If we are to evolve as a civilization, it will be because we prioritize the *vagina*.

    *(**NAN** knows exactly what is happening.)*

TED. *(Vagina.)* Yup.

DR. PAP. *(Vagina.)* Our work on care for the *vagina*, here at Cornell, will ensure that diseases of the *vagina*, the world over, will be eradicated for the benefit of the *vagina* everywhere. *(Indicating* **NAN**.*)* Including your own.

> *(Awkward.)*

TED. Yaaaaaaay

> *(So awkward.)*

NAN.	**TED**.
Why don't you go to work.	I should probably go.

TED. It was wonderful to meet you sir.

DR. PAP. I hear we are having dinner together.

TED. Very much looking forward to it.

DR. PAP. Me too. Bye bye now.

TED. Okay. Bye.

> *(Sensing he didn't take the gold medal,* **TED** *leaves.* **DR. PAP** *immediately sets about his work.* **NAN** *watches him.)*

NAN. That wasn't necessary.

DR. PAP. *(Feigning innocence.)* What?

NAN. Vagina vagina vagina.

DR. PAP. Oh, come now.

NAN. You were talking down to him.

DR. PAP. I was just teasing.

NAN. Ted is one of us.

DR. PAP. Well now there you're wrong.

NAN. Why do you say that?

DR. PAP. I just know.

NAN. That's not fair.

DR. PAP. That's the way it is in our field; you'd better get used to it. And you must admit, it was a little fun to see him squirm.

(She will not admit.)

NAN. Is your wife one of us?

DR. PAP. Mache? Of course. I couldn't have done what I've done without Mache.

NAN. Then why are her slides in the trash?

(This stops him.)

The slides she brought to the lab. They're in the trash this morning.

DR. PAP. That – was a misunderstanding.

NAN. Why would she bring slides that you then throw away?

DR. PAP. Nan, that is a very – complicated matter between Mache and myself. I'm sorry that she involved you – and – now that is all I wish to say on the matter. Let us begin our work.

(He moves on. After a moment, she reluctantly follows.)

Go ahead and examine these slides, mark what you think is abnormal, you have the pens there, and we'll go over them together.

(She sets herself at the microscope.)

NAN. *(Trying to find her question.)* Is it strange for you?

DR. PAP. Is what strange?

NAN. I don't know. Looking at someone's vagina.

DR. PAP. You mean does it feel sexual...many men have asked me that, you know. Faculty parties with bourbon and cigars, but you are the first woman. The answer is <u>no</u>. It is not sexual. All that goes away, and the vagina becomes *medical.*

NAN. ...

DR. PAP. *(That twinkle again.)* Are you as disappointed as the men?

> *(She blushes. She looks into the microscope.)*

NAN. There are so many...

DR. PAP. Cells? About 100,000 cells per smear. Finding the cancerous ones is literally like looking for a needle in a haystack.

NAN. *(Looking.)* It's like – a night sky.

DR. PAP. You know, that's exactly what I said. *(He watches her work for a moment.)* Nan.

> *(She looks up.)*

I think we're going to be a wonderful team.

> *(Blackout.)*

Four

*(Another day. **NAN** and **DR. PAP** are at the chalkboard analyzing drawings of several types of cells. They are sharing a box of raisins. She is flush with a discovery.)*

NAN. So you know how some of the koilocytes are bi-nucleated? –

DR. PAP. Of course. These raisins are amazing.

NAN. I thought they'd make a nice snack.

DR. PAP. Affirmative.

NAN. So okay, here's the thing –

DR. PAP. Okay! –

NAN. I've noticed that many of them have a kind of – I don't know what to call it – a kind of *halo* around them.

DR. PAP. Yes.

> *(She puts a slide on the stage of the microscope.)*

NAN. I marked it with blue.

> *(As he looks in.)*

DR. PAP. And what do you make of that? What could that halo be about?

NAN. Well at first I thought it could just be the glycogen –

DR. PAP. Yes.

NAN. *(Intense.)* But then I thought, what if it's the cancer? What if that space between the nucleus and the halo is the cancer?

> *(He's testing her.)*

DR. PAP. That's an interesting idea. Tell me more...

> *(She suddenly senses the test.)*

NAN. You know about this already. The halo.

DR. PAP. *(Concedes.)* I do. Yes. *(Very serious.)* But Nan, I am *very* impressed that you noticed this. I'm serious. Now go on. Tell me what you've observed.

> *(A moment where she realizes he genuinely wants her opinion on this. That feels good.)*

NAN. Well, when you look at this slide here, you can see –

> *(Suddenly* **TED** *bounds in.)*

TED. Surprise!

> *(Both* **DR. PAP** *and* **NAN** *just look at him blankly.)*

Ha! Hi!

NAN. *(Not pleased to see him, and not hiding it.)* – ? – Hi.

TED. *(Pulling out a bouquet of flowers.)* I brought you daisies! Aren't they pretty?!

NAN. Gerbers.

TED. What?

NAN. They're Gerbers.

TED. Oh, whatever – Here!

NAN. ...Thank you.

TED. You like them?

NAN. It's very sweet of you.

> *(***NAN*** *puts the Gerbers in an empty beaker on the lab table.* **TED** *enters the room more, hands on his hips.)*

TED. Hi!

DR. PAP. Hello Ted.

TED. I was hoping to steal Nan for a minute. I also brought some flowers. Mmm, these raisins look good. May I?

NAN. Uh. Sure.

(*He pops a raisin in his mouth, grinning.*)

TED. Yum! So! – are you able to take a quick break?

NAN. Well, no, we're kind of busy at the moment.

TED. Oh. What're you guys up to?

NAN. We're working.

TED. Whatcha working on?

NAN. Oh you know. Cancer.

TED. Right.

NAN. Of the vagina.

TED. (*Vagina.*)... Right.

(**NAN** *does not look at* **DR. PAP**. *But he watches.*)

NAN. (*Vagina.*) These are slides of vaginal fluid that we're analyzing under the microscope.

TED. (*Trying to stay in it.*) Uh huh

NAN. (*Vagina.*) So we take a sample from the vagina – well the inner cervix and the outer cervix, which is inside the vagina.

TED. (*Vagina.*) Mm.

NAN. And we smear it here. To see if we find any cancer.

TED. Wow.

NAN. Cancer in the vagina. That's what we do.

TED. Sounds good...Great.

> *(Beat. Getting he's not welcome.)*

Well, I guess I'll leave you to it. I'm heading over to work for a meeting, so maybe we can just – talk later? Or –?

DR. PAP. Nan, if you need to take a break.

NAN. I don't need a break, we can talk later, right Ted?

DR. PAP. But if your husband needs to –

NAN. No no, Ted's not that kind of husband.

TED. What kind of husband?

NAN. The kind that would pull the husband card to take a break during his wife's important work if she feels it's not a good time to take a break.

TED. *(Means it.)* Oh. No, I'm definitely not that kind of husband.

DR. PAP. Alright.

NAN. Okay, so –

TED. Yeah, okay.

DR. PAP. You have the address for tonight, right Ted?

TED. *(Patting his breast pocket.)* I do. Oh! *(Realizes they'll go to the dinner separately.)* I'll just – I'll meet you there...?

NAN. That'd be great, thank you honey.

DR. PAP. Just park outside the house. The one with the Dogwood in front.

TED. *(Profoundly disconcerted.)* Alrighty. See you tonight.

NAN. *(Kisses **TED**'s cheek.)* Bye honey.

(**TED** *leaves. A conspiratorial silence between*
NAN *and* **DR. PAP** *as they resume.*)

DR. PAP. Where were we?

NAN. This next slide. Look.

(**NAN** *puts the slide under the microscope.* **DR.
PAP** *looks.*)

This is from someone who is stage four. As you can
see...

DR. PAP. (*Looking.*) ...It's full of halos.

NAN. Yes.

(**DR. PAP** *keeps looking.*)

DR. PAP. It's terrible to imagine, isn't it? This is from a
young mother of three.

NAN. (*Swallows gravely.*) – Yes.

(*He looks for a long time, takes some notes.
She watches and waits. This seems to open up
an anxiety in her. A quiet, dark one.*)

Dr. Pap?

DR. PAP. (*Doesn't look up.*) Mm?

NAN. (*Carefully.*) Dr. Pap. What are the early symptoms
of cancer?

DR. PAP. What kind of cancer?

NAN. The cervix. The ovaries. The lower body...in general...

(*He looks up.*)

DR. PAP. Why do you ask?

NAN. (*Uneasy under his gaze.*) ...

DR. PAP. Do you know someone?

NAN. Do I know someone?

DR. PAP. Someone with cancer...

> (**NAN** *swallows.*)

NAN. Ted's grandmother. Ted's grandmother died of cancer.

DR. PAP. Ah.

> (*Beat. It seems like that's the end of it. Then –*)

NAN. And my Aunt Jenny.

DR. PAP. I see.

NAN. (*Slowly, each name like the toll of a heavy bell.*) And my Aunt Carol.

And cousin Eleanor.

My friend Maggie.

And her mother.

And her aunt.

Carol Ann the organist.

The postmaster's wife, Elizabeth.

> (**DR. PAP** *sits back and takes in this sizable list as it slowly unspools.*)

Miss Marie, my elementary school teacher.

Our neighbor, Rebecca Waters.

Mrs. Putnam, down the road (though I don't really *know* her...)

The midwife, Ruth Ann.

And her sister Mary Jean.

DR. PAP. You know all these women with cancer...

NAN. I do.

DR. PAP. Then you understand.

NAN. Understand...?

DR. PAP. Our work.

NAN. *(Gravely.)* I do.

DR. PAP. Why didn't you mention any of this? In your cover letter.

NAN. I don't know. I didn't want to be too personal.

DR. PAP. Science should always be personal. It's too important to be anything else.

> *(A beat.)*

We don't really know the early symptoms of cancer. Until now, the cancer is discovered so late that it has spread very deep into the area, so there is a lot of pain. But as we continue to discover the cancer *sooner*, we may find that there are indeed *warning signs*.

NAN. Warning signs?

DR. PAP. Symptoms that until now have not been connected to the cancer, but are in fact the cancer revealing itself. The body trying to communicate that something is very wrong.

The body always asks to be seen.

> *(He regards her for an uncomfortably long moment. She feels the weight of her secret. Then he suddenly gets up, opens a drawer, and hands her a key.)*

Here.

NAN. What's this?

DR. PAP. A key.

NAN. What for?

DR. PAP. Don't be thick, it's for the lab. I want you to have your own copy.

NAN. But my contract is only –

DR. PAP. Oh nonsense, just take it. So you can come and go as you see fit.

NAN. *(Moved.)* I don't know what to say.

DR. PAP. Don't say anything. Just get back to work.

> *(***NAN*** *nods. Puts the key in the pocket of her skirt. Then resumes her seat at an adjacent microscope. A few moments as they sit like that, working. After several beats, she looks up. Despite the gravity of the conversation they just had, she feels a kind of happiness that is different from any other happiness she's experienced before. Then she puts her face back to the microscope. And works.)*
>
> *(Blackout.)*

Five

*(The home of Dr. Pap and Mache. Not ostentatious, but comfortable and well kept. Some amazing Greek dish is in the oven. **MACHE** and **TED** are at the piano, drinks nearby – maybe their second. **TED** is performing a hymn "Leaning on the Everlasting Arms.")*

TED. *(Uptempo, with great gusto.)*
WHAT A FELLOWSHIP, WHAT A JOY DIVINE
LEANING ON THE EVERLASTING ARMS
WHAT A BLESSEDNESS, WHAT A PEACE IS MINE
LEANING ON THE EVERLASTING ARMS
LEANING, LEANING
SAFE AND SECURE FROM ALL ALARMS
LEANING, LEANING
LEANING ON THE EVERLASTING ARMS!

MACHE. That's catchy!

TED. I like it! It rouses the spirit!

(He resumes and she joins him, maybe sashays around the room. Her voice is loud and plain.)

TED & MACHE. *(Singing.)*
LEANING, LEANING, LEANING ON THE EVERLASTING ARMS!

(They finish with a big laugh.)

MACHE. Who needs our spouses?

TED. Not us! Well, maybe me...

MACHE. You'll get used to it. And you can come play for me anytime.

(**DR. PAP** *and* **NAN** *can be heard at the door.*
TED *stops.*)

TED. Oh there they are!

MACHE. Ah yes, they always eventually come home.

(**DR. PAP** *and* **NAN** *enter.*)

DR. PAP. Here we are, here we are, very sorry!

NAN. Forgive us, we got caught up.

MACHE. I remember what that is like. Come in, come in!

(*Coats, hats, hellos, etc.* **NAN** *crosses to* **TED**
and gives him a peck on the cheek.)

NAN. Were you singing?

TED. We were!

MACHE. Ted was teaching me a song.

TED. A hymn actually, I was playing for Mache.

DR. PAP. What is this song?

TED. Oh, the hymn? It's called "*Leaning on the Everlasting
Arms.*"

MACHE. It rouses the spirit.

DR. PAP. And what is this word you're using?

TED. What word? Oh, hymn?

DR. PAP. Him? You call it a Him? Interesting. Are there
also songs you call a Her, just to even it out?

TED. (*Not necessarily fully following.*) Uh...?

DR. PAP. Maybe if a song is for Jesus you call it a Him, and
if a song is for Mary you call it a Her.

TED. Oh! Haha. You're thinking *Him.* H-i-m. No no,
hymn. H-y-m-n.

DR. PAP. Oooooh, now I see. Hymn. Not Him. Yes.

*(Is **DR. PAP** fucking with him?)*

MACHE. Watch out, Ted. Remember – this is a man who spent years with an eye dropper in a guinea pig's vagina.

*(**TED** spits up his drink.)*

TED. An eye dropper in a guinea pig's vagina?

DR. PAP. *(Vagina.)* Good for you, Ted!

TED. Is that *true*?

DR. PAP. Of course it's true, that's how I discovered the Pap smear.

TED. *(Appalled.)* What – was that?

NAN. Ted.

DR. PAP. What was what?

TED. *(He struggles to put words into a question.)* I mean, what did that – do?

DR. PAP. It revealed the logic of the female reproductive system, that's what it did.

MACHE. It also made one smell a little funny.

*(**TED** spits up again.)*

TED. Hanfry, I'm a making a terrible mess of myself.

DR. PAP. That's right, make fun of me, how original. Have you been hanging out with the faculty at Cornell?

MACHE. You know I haven't.

DR. PAP. Except to drop off lab samples.

MACHE. *(Moving right on, grinning to **TED**.)* He used to come home from the lab, this was twenty years ago, 1932 or so. I had no friends, and he would come home smelling of formaldehyde and guinea pig vagina.

TED. Wow.

MACHE. I would have dinner prepared, but first – he had to take a shower. That was the rule!

TED. I get it!

NAN. *(Redirecting.)* Dr. Pap, what an amazing library.

DR. PAP. Thank you. Yes. We carried most of it on our backs from Europe.

MACHE. *(To* **NAN.***)* Literally. *(Pointing to her back.)* I still have the scars.

DR. PAP. Mache, why don't you give Nan a little tour. Of the house...

NAN. Oh I'd like that very much.

MACHE. Alright. Shall I show her "the lab?"

NAN. You have a lab in the house?

DR. PAP. No no, we don't have a lab, there's no lab, she's joking. Nan, now you will see how a scientist can live! If she applies herself! *(Taking* **MACHE***'s wine.)* Alright, off you go.

MACHE. *(Pointing to a door.)* Alright. This is the restroom in case you want to powder your nose.

NAN. Oh. I don't powder.

MACHE. Really?

TED. True fact! Nan does not even *own* powder.

MACHE. *(A fresh regard for* **NAN.***)* Maybe we are going to be friends after all.

NAN. I would like that.

> *(And with that* **NAN** *and* **MACHE** *leave to tour the house.)*

DR. PAP. In Greece we have a saying – toso o psaras ta psaria kai.

Both the fisherman and the fish.

TED. ...Sorry?

DR. PAP. Women. Both the fisherman and the fish.

> (**TED** *contemplates that for a disturbed moment.*)

TED. I don't really get it.

DR. PAP. That's okay. Let me give you a piece of advice, Ted. If you can bear with an old fool who has studied the interiority of women for over three decades: There is an entire galaxy in there.

TED. In...?

DR. PAP. Women.

TED. An entire galaxy.

DR. PAP. Yes.

TED. Huh.

DR. PAP. When you look at Nan –

TED. Yes

DR. PAP. What do you see?

TED. When I look at Nan

DR. PAP. Yes

TED. What do I *see*...?

> (**TED** *very earnestly considers this, and this is very Ted. He takes everything straight on. Always open. He accepts whatever is put before him with hearty New England optimism.*)

I see...my best friend. My equal. I see Nan. Just as she is. Tall, true Nan.

DR. PAP. This is not good.

TED. No?

DR. PAP. No. Tall, true Nan?

TED. Sure.

DR. PAP. No. I mean, yes. Tall, true Nan, yes. But it's a mistake to believe that women are as they appear. This is not only false, it is insulting.

TED. Insulting.

DR. PAP. Yes

TED. Insulting??

DR. PAP. Listen: Everything that is all around you – the trees, the molecules of the air, the light, the fibers of this couch, the color of nail varnish, the sound of a pencil on paper, the creatures of the ocean. All these things were made from the materials of our universe. Somehow. Our minds cannot possibly understand how this complex and miraculous planet we live on, and everything that lives on it, came from the various materials of our universe, but it is true. You understand?

TED. Our miraculous planet.

DR. PAP. Yes.

TED. Came from the materials of our universe.

DR. PAP. Yes.

TED. Okay.

DR. PAP. It is the same with women. It is the *same with women*! Everything that I am, that you are, our hands, our hair, our respiratory system, the tiny neurons of our memory...all of this was made from the materials inside a woman.

TED. ...And a man. The materials of a woman *and a man*.

DR. PAP. Sure sure, the little *sperm*, whoo hoo. No: The entire planet that is you, that is me, that is Nan, that is Abraham Lincoln, that is Renoir, came from the materials that are inside a woman. So when you look at a woman – you see your partner, your equal –

TED. Of course

DR. PAP. And you are wrong. There is a *galaxy* in there. Inside Nan. Inside Mache. Inside every woman. It is willful ignorance to count yourself equal to *that*.

(*Beat.*)

TED. I find that a very dangerous point of view.

DR. PAP. Do you?

TED. I do.

DR. PAP. Why dangerous, why do you say dangerous?

(*This isn't some speech* **TED** *has prepared, he's finding it as he goes.*)

TED. Look, this is a common idea – women are *different*, men are one thing, women are another. But it is my observation that the logic of women as *different* is the first step to *treating women differently*. And frankly, I find it particularly chilling to link such reverence to *her reproductive system*. Yes, women can make a baby, and that's a miracle, a miraculous thing, but at the same time, she IS simply herself. If women are regarded the same as men, no more and no less, then they must be granted the same rights as men. In all areas of civilized life – the work place, the church, the state. Yes, *it just so happens* that women can make a baby. (*A little threatening.*) But maybe it also *just so happens* that you are very good with an *eye dropper* and *I can run a six-minute mile*.

(Quick beat.)

Regardless of what we can *do*, you are still just Dr. Pap and I am still just Ted Day, and we have the same rights and protections. The minute you start adding little addendums – like she is Nan *but she can make a baby* – suddenly extra rules and regulations can be added – I'm talking LAWS – so the woman starts to lose control of her *individuality*. If she is just a PERSON, like a man is just a person, she just might stand a chance of attaining equality.

*(**DR. PAP** regards him. He underestimated him.)*

DR. PAP. I understand you Ted. I do. Of course women are equal to men. I could not do the work I do without my wife, and there must be nothing, nothing that impedes the role of women in public life.

TED. Her abilities must be granted the same access as men!

DR. PAP. Hear hear!

TED. Amen!

DR. PAP. Play ball!

(Quick beat.)

But when the dust has settled...when women are properly installed next to men – when the great work to achieve this is through... Imagine before you, if you can, the female reproductive system: the fallopian tubes, the cervix, the womb...place it firmly in your mind, and then imagine that somehow, in there, an entire consciousness comes to being...and then look into the eyes of every woman you encounter, and your Nan, and see if you can honestly say that you are as much as they. Cocktail?

TED. Make it a double.

>(**MACHE** *and* **NAN** *re-enter, chuckling. They carry glasses of Greek digestif and it's clear they've been enjoying it.*)

DR. PAP. How was the tour?

MACHE. Excellent!

NAN. I'm trying this Greek drink – Ouzo! It tastes like licorice!

TED. Wow.

MACHE. Show Ted your new trick.

TED.	**DR. PAP.**
Your what?	Oh dear.

NAN. *(Giggling.)* Oh my gosh.

TED. What new trick?

>(**NAN** *burps a Greek word.*)

NAN. *(Burped.)* "Nostimo" *(Just fucking tickled with herself.)* It means delicious!

MACHE. Nostimo!

TED. *(A little shocked, but rolling with it.)* Ha!

DR. PAP. Mache you are corrupting my lab partner.

MACHE. Ted would you like to try some Ouzo?

TED. Sure!

>(**MACHE** *pours* **TED** *some Ouzo.*)

NAN. It's *(Burped.)* "nostimo"

MACHE. Nostimo!

>(*More laughter.* **TED** *can't help but join in.*)

TED. Yum!

MACHE. Everything Greek is delicious.

DR. PAP. Except the economy.

NAN. So what were you two conspiring about while we were gone?

DR. PAP. *(Preparing drinks.)* What else? Women!

> *(Somehow* **NAN** *and* **MACHE** *hear that the exact same way.)*

NAN. Did you hear that, Mache?

MACHE. Our husbands were conspiring about women.

NAN. That's interesting.

MACHE. I agree.

NAN. Do you?

MACHE. Our husbands conspiring about women? It's very interesting.

NAN. Or –

MACHE. Or –

NAN. Not interesting at all.

MACHE. *Not interesting at all. (Ching!)*

TED. Well now, in fairness, we were discussing the *equality* of women.

NAN. Oh, well in *that case* –

MACHE. Oooohh –

NAN. If you were discussing the *equality* of women –

MACHE. Sure

NAN. Then maybe it's –?

MACHE. No.

NAN. Nope. Still not that interesting.

MACHE. Dinner will be ready in ten minutes.

> (**MACHE** *exits to the kitchen.* **NAN** *trips on the edge of a carpet.*)

TED. You alright?

NAN. I'm fine.

TED. *(Chuckling, covering for her.)* This one. I call her my little Charlie Chaplain. Brilliant and prone to spills.

NAN. *(Ignoring.)* You have a lovely home, Dr. Pap.

DR. PAP. How's *your* home coming along?

> (*Slight ripple passes through* **TED** *and* **NAN.**)

NAN. Oh. Well.

TED. We haven't really had much time.

DR. PAP. Ah.

NAN. We're getting there. It takes time to make a home.

TED. It does.

DR. PAP. Well, this is the science life.

TED. Is it? I mean, is there ever a point that it lets up? When the hours become, I don't know, more regular?

NAN. *(Quietly.)* Ted.

DR. PAP. That depends what you consider more regular.

TED. I mean, should she want to...find other...like at a good hospital or something.

DR. PAP. Yes, once Nan finishes her training she could work for a hospital somewhere. Examine slides and make diagnostic notes for the doctors to interpret. But the world doesn't need people to make notes

for doctors. The world needs *research*. Early detection.
A *cure*.

> (**TED** *and* **NAN** *are quiet.* **NAN***'s face is very
> flushed.*)

TED. *(Seeing* **NAN.***)* I'm sorry – have I – ...?

> (**MACHE** *returns from the kitchen.*)

MACHE. What are we talking about?

NAN. *(An anger simmering beneath.)* What are we always
talking about? The vagina.

TED. Nan.

NAN. Yes you are. *(To* **TED.***)* You're talking about my vagina
to make our family. *(To* **DR. PAP.***)* And you're talking
about my vagina to work to save other vaginas.

TED. Honey.

NAN. What I find so ironic is that neither of you has one.
I'm the one who has a vagina. And Mache too as far as
I can tell.

MACHE. Affirmative.

NAN. And you have no idea what that is like.

TED. What what is like?

NAN. Having a vagina, Ted! What it's like to have a vagina!

DR. PAP. Would you like to tell us?

> *(Beat.* **TED** *looks from* **DR. PAP** *to* **NAN.***)*

NAN. *(Maybe slightly unprepared.)* Well – just as a
physical attribute...it's really not that bad.

MACHE. I'd agree.

NAN. It aches when you have your period. Your period is a
whole – *thing* –

MACHE. Those were the days!

NAN. But mostly, on a daily basis, having a vagina is really perfectly fine.

MACHE. Well. It can be itchy.

NAN. It can, Mache. That's a good point, it can be itchy. But all in all I'd say I'm a fan. Of having a vagina. I like the fact that it's private in there, that no one else can tell what's going on in my vagina.

MACHE. (*Yuck.*) As opposed to the *penis*. Which –

NAN. (*So out there.*) Exactly.

MACHE. (*So predictable.*) Yes.

NAN. And I like the fact that if I ever really really needed to, I could maybe *hide* something in there.

TED. In your vagina.

NAN. Yes that's right, Ted! I could hide something in my vagina.

TED. You could??

NAN. Absolutely.

MACHE. Sure

NAN. And you would have *no idea*! You would have *no idea* there was something hiding in my vagina! It's like my own private little *cave*. And I like that it is both very very small, and also incredibly *spacious* in there. Like it's actually a portal to another *world*.

MACHE. PLANETS.

NAN. Another *dimension*.

MACHE. OLYMPUS.

NAN. Sometimes – especially after sex – it can feel like a gaping...weepy...

WOUND.

MACHE. Yes.

NAN. And then sometimes...?

MACHE. It's more like a dark...

NAN. Arid...

MACHE. TOMB.

(A shift.)

NAN. But in a *symbolic* way? ...Having a vagina is very confusing.

*(**MACHE** is nodding, grave.)*

It's this thing I'm supposed to *protect* all the time.

Uh oh, look out for your vagina, don't accidentally end up burned at the STAKE or something. Which makes it really hard to *enjoy*. It's like a rhinoceros and their tusk. Hunters are always looking to cut off your tusk. It is very valuable. And through no fault of your own, you were born with one. So you're always on the run. At risk. In danger. Because everyone wants a piece of your tusk. But it's MY TUSK. On the inside. It's my tusk on the inside.

(Beat. Or not.)

MACHE. And then imagine your tusk suddenly CHANGES! You can't count on it anymore. And people treat you differently. You spent your whole life paying for your tusk. Being *less* because of your tusk. And then your tusk is gone, and suddenly you're *even less*.

NAN. That's terrible.

MACHE. Affirmative.

(Subtle shift.)

NAN.   This whole – thing. The whole lower body – is a mystery. Like those pictures of gas clouds or constellations where stars are born. Imagine if you had one of those *inside you*. You're just as shocked as everyone else! But you're still just – *you*.

> (**TED**'s *mouth is agape, disturbed, very moved.*)

DR. PAP.   This is very interesting for me. Because you are right. As you say, I have been studying the vagina for a very long time, but perhaps I have much to learn.

> (*They all sit in a thoughtful silence.*)

MACHE.   (*Somewhat out of nowhere.*) I need a tall young man to reach a very high shelf.

TED.   (*Please God give me a task.*) That I can do.

> (*He leaves with* **MACHE** *back into the kitchen.* **DR. PAP** *watches* **NAN**. *The tone darkens further in that silence.*)

DR. PAP.   I want you to be very honest with me.

NAN.   ...About –?

DR. PAP.   The falls you take.

The discomfort in your legs.

The balance issues.

Shall I go on?

NAN.   (*Absolutely crushed, no idea what to say.*) ...

DR. PAP.   Did you think I wouldn't notice? I am a scientist, Nan.

> (**NAN** *shakes her head, trying to contain her emotion.*)

Does Ted know?

NAN. *(Absolutely crushed.)* He knows, he just...doesn't know how much it...

DR. PAP. Nan...?

(It's a huge deal to admit it.)

NAN. There's something wrong. With me. Something – is happening. I can't rely on my legs – I don't...something is wrong.

DR. PAP. Have you seen a doctor?

(Her head keeps shaking. It's difficult to speak.)

NAN. They don't know. No one knows. What it is.

(A grave silence.)

MACHE. Dinner is served!

DR. PAP. We will continue this later.

*(**TED** and **MACHE** re-enter with food. **MACHE** notices how connected **DR. PAP** and **NAN** are. They all make their way to the table.)*

TED. Just sit anywhere?

DR. PAP. Ted, you are over there. Nan, you sit by me.

TED. Alright.

*(**TED** gives **NAN** a squeeze. She unconsciously pulls away. He hesitates, then sits.)*

Shall we say grace?

MACHE. Grace. Hahahaha.

TED. That's a good one. I meant –

MACHE. Don't you think Grace is a better name than Nan?

TED. Uh –

MACHE. Nan is so plain, so – I don't know – in Greek we say "stereos" – solid –

Whereas Grace – Grace makes *promises* don't you think?

TED. I don't know what *promises* you're referring to, but I think Nan is the perfect name.

MACHE. This is just like a husband, isn't it?

TED. *(Flustered.)* I don't – I'm not –

NAN. *(Trying to be helpful.)* Ted, why don't you just say grace.

TED. What, you're saying you prefer Grace now?

NAN. The *blessing* Ted, say the *blessing*.

TED. *(He just can't win.)* Oh hanfry. Yes. Let us pray.

> *(They bow their heads.)*

Heavenly Father. We thank you for this food we are about to receive. Let it fortify us to do Your good work.

NAN. *(Thinking that's the end.)* Amen.

> *(But poor **TED** is really wrestling with a troubled heart.)*

TED. Lord we also ask...that You – guide us – in our most intimate matters of the heart. Protect our bonds of love that we hold so dear.

Keep our sights on Your great plan for our family and our togetherness.

And if there is anyone – who is mad at us – for any reason – that we surely didn't intend – please help them forgive us – and...

> *(That thought seems to run out of gas...)*

In the name of the Father, the Son, and the Holy Spirit. Amen.

(Murmurs of Amen from the table.)

MACHE. *(Means it.)* That was a good grace, Ted.

DR. PAP. Well. I think we should get some food in our stomachs.

(They eat.)

NAN. Mache this is delicious.

MACHE. It's Lamb Kleftiko. We had this dish the night we met, do you remember Georgios?

DR. PAP. I do. Mache is a wonderful cook. It's one of her many talents.

NAN. How did you meet?

DR. PAP. *(Glad for a chance to lift things.)* Ah! Yes! This is a wonderful story –: A group of young people from the village were going on a hike and we were among them. All the women wore the wrong shoes for the hike. It wasn't their fault, this was what women wore, mind you, and the terrain was very rocky, very difficult. All the women were complaining, they were hot, they had blisters, but – not a word from Mache. She was silent, she just hiked. At one point, I looked down and I saw that her shoe had a hole in it, and she was bleeding from her foot. But she never complained. Not once! I knew then that she was a very special kind of person. Someone who would understand me, who could endure a life in science. Someone who could be my partner.

(It has moved him to recount this story.)

I would like to propose a toast. To the future. Which owes a very very great deal to the past.

ALL. *(Toasting.)* To the future.

TED. Actually. On that note. I have an announcement to make! I got some good news today. I was offered a parish! In Lunenberg, outside of Boston.

It's the perfect place for us – liberal, progressive. Anyway. I'm very pleased.

NAN. *(Completely shocked.)* When did you find out?

TED. Today. That's why I stopped by. With the flowers.

NAN. You should've told me.

TED. *(Sincere.)* I tried, I – I didn't want to be that kind of husband.

DR. PAP. Congratulations, Ted.

TED. Thank you! We start next month. Which should work perfectly, give Nan enough time to finish her contract here. I negotiated specifically that her commitment here be honored.

> *(Beat.)*

DR. PAP. Oh. You're leaving?

NAN.	**TED.**
Not necessarily.	It's disappointing –

> *(Beat.)*

TED. What?

NAN. I could – commute, or... I don't know, I'm just hearing this myself...

TED. But –

NAN. Ted, I'm not – we just – we just need to discuss everything.

> *(Beat.)*

MACHE. *(Toast.)* To discussing everything!

(They wanly toast. She suddenly sings a Greek drinking song.*)

DR. PAP. *(Trying to cover, keep it light.)* It's a Greek song of celebration.

*(**MACHE** continues singing.)*

DR. PAP. Okay Mache. Maybe you're not feeling well.

MACHE. I'm very well, look how well I sing.

(She continues singing.)

DR. PAP. Alright, why don't you lie down on the bed for a few minutes.

MACHE. Ooooooh BEDTIME! Is it time to get a sample?

DR. PAP. Mache, enough. You are drunk.

MACHE. *(To **NAN** and **TED**.)* Did you know that I was his subject?

DR. PAP. *(Head in hands.)* Mache

NAN. You were what?

MACHE. His subject. His first human subject.

NAN. *(To **DR. PAP**.)* Is that true?

MACHE. Ooooh she didn't know. Ahhhh haha – yes indeed – For years and years, from the beginning, I was his only human subject. I was his guinea pig! And I loved it. I was happy! Here look.

(She unloads a box of slides onto the table. Just like the box of slides she brought to the lab earlier. Everyone jumps up.)

---

* A license to produce *Nan And The Lower Body* does not include a performance license for any third-party or copyrighted music. Licensees should create an original composition or use music in the public domain. For further information, please see the Music and Third-Party Materials Use Note on page iii.

TED. Hanfry!

MACHE. This is my vaginal fluid! Quite something, eh? Take a good look, Nan – this is what a life with Dr. Pap looks like. *Until he doesn't need you anymore.*

DR. PAP. *(Sadly.)* Mache.

MACHE. *(Her despair unmaskable.)* Now I'm OLD. My tusk is gone. I'm alllllllll USED UP.

DR. PAP. *(Intimate.)* My love, you *know this*. We can't use the samples if they are menopausal.

It's just science, my koukla. Nothing more.

MACHE. *(Drunk, weeping now.)* Did it ever occur to you that I was crying? That's why I was silent? My foot was bleeding and I felt a fool woman for those shoes, and I was walking in silence because if I spoke I would *sob*. But you only saw my silence. You didn't see my tears.

DR. PAP. *(Cradling her, truly truly.)* Oh my Mache. My Mache. What a fool I have been. How much you have done for me. With me. We've walked a long road together, haven't we. Remember the old days? – when we had no heat and we had to go to bed right after dinner. We'd sing the little song, you remember?

> *(He hums it to her, it is a sweet little song and somehow there's humor in it between them. She remembers. Eventually sings along. It's as if there is no one else in the room.*)*

Come my koukla. Come to bed.

> *(Tenderly, they head towards the bedroom. Sometime throughout all this, **NAN**'s leg has*

---

* A license to produce *Nan And The Lower Body* does not include a performance license for any third-party or copyrighted music. Licensees should create an original composition or use music in the public domain. For further information, please see the Music and Third-Party Materials Use Note on page iii.

begun to hurt terribly. She holds herself up, clutching it. **TED** *watches them go, surveying the spilled slides.)*

TED. Jesus God. *His wife is his human subject???* It's – it's...

> *(He sees her. Rushes to her.)*

What's wrong? Are you alright?

NAN. It's my – my legs.

TED. I thought you said it was better.

NAN. I don't – know –

TED. You're working too much, Nan, you're exhausted. You heard what he said, this is the job! The hours never let up!

NAN. You just don't like him!

TED. Come on, Nan! I believe in science! I believe in YOU! But this *(Meaning Dr. Pap, this job.)* – this is too much. I don't even... Look at me. Is this the life you want, Nan? Truly? Tell me. Do you want this? For you? For us?

> *(**NAN** is trembling.)*

(Tenderly.) My love. Talk to me.

> *(**TED** makes his case. This is what they've always wanted.)*

Lunenberg is a wonderful town. Forests on all sides. You can get a great job with this work you've done. Your talents will thrive. Isn't that what we've planned? Isn't that our dream? For us? For little Sara and Mark? Nan. *Grace.* Please.

NAN. *Something is wrong with me.* Something is wrong.

> *(**TED** stops. Understands something for the first time. She continues –)*

What if I can't work?

What if it spreads up my legs,

Through my pelvis and my arms...

What if I can only sign my name with my left hand?

What if I have to be lifted on and off the toilet?

What if we have to live with our daughter's family

And our grandchildren are afraid of us

Because every morning while they pour their cereal

They can smell our medications

And urine?

What if they tip toe around the house

To avoid our frail, needy gaze...?

> *(A grave beat.)*

TED. *(Absorbing the enormity of what she just revealed.)* Even if all that happens...I am with you. We will face whatever comes.

Together.

> *(**NAN** knows it's true. The wheels in her mind are spinning.)*

NAN. Alright. But first you must let me do something.

> *(Blackout.)*

Six

*(Hours later, back at the lab. It's the middle of the night. **NAN** enters and waits. After a moment, **DR. PAP** enters too. Silence for a moment.)*

DR. PAP. You're leaving. Aren't you?

NAN. Yes.

> *(That sets in.)*

DR. PAP. The Dean said this would happen. When I wanted to hire you. He said a woman will always choose her family.

NAN. *(So difficult to say.)* I'm sorry, Dr. Pap. I know you had great hopes for me. And this has been – wonderful. Truly it has. But I want other things for my life.

DR. PAP. So what are we doing here?

> *(Grave beat.)*

NAN. You said yourself we don't know the early symptoms of cancer. Who can tell me but you? Where else can I turn? You have to help me.

> *(A beat. He comprehends what she wants.)*

DR. PAP. I could lose my job, Nan. My job. You called me here in the middle of the night. I came. I care for you Nan, truly I do. But I cannot – I cannot do that.

NAN. Please.

DR. PAP. No! What about Ted?

NAN. Ted and I made a deal. I need to see my cells. My self. Dr. Pap. Look at me. Please.

> *(Beat.)*

DR. PAP. Very well. Put this on.

> *(He sets up the table, the speculum, while she puts on the robe. He puts on gloves and a surgical mask. When he turns back, she is just standing there. A beat between them.)*

NAN. I don't know...what to...*do*.

DR. PAP. Take my hand.

> *(She takes his hand. Helps her to the table.)*

(Very gently, with care.) Please, sit here. You'll put your feet in these stirrups. That's right.

> *(She nods.)*

Good. Then when you're ready, you slide down towards me.

> *(She puts her feet in the stirrups and slides down.)*

A little further. A little further. Good.

Are you alright?

NAN. Yes.

> *(**DR. PAP** sits on a stool in front of her and turns on an examination light. If these two people have become close over the course of the last few weeks, it is not evident now. He is pure professional and she is his patient. Except when he is describing what he is doing to her, everything is conducted with somber silence. In real time. I want the audience to sit through as realistic of a Pap smear as possible. Ladies, you've probably been through it many times. Gentlemen, you've probably never even imagined it. Now we'll all sit and watch it. **DR. PAP** continues.)*

DR. PAP. Okay Nan. I'm going to insert the speculum.

NAN. Is it going to hurt?

DR. PAP. It will be uncomfortable, but there shouldn't be any *pain*. Ready?

NAN. Yes.

DR. PAP. Take a deep breath.

> *(Perhaps a soft "puh" from* **NAN** *as he gently inserts the speculum.)*

Try to relax. Good.

> *(She does.)*

Now I'm inserting the spatula.

You'll feel me collecting the tissue from the inside and the outside of the cervix, the transition zone.

NAN. Both endocervical cells and squamous cells.

DR. PAP. *(A small smile of pride at his protégé.)* Correct.

> *(It is very quiet. And very intimate. It is clear she is physically uncomfortable, though there is no pain.)*

We're almost through here.

> *(He withdraws the wooden spatula and smears the sample onto a slide.)*

Now I'm going to remove the speculum.

Alright. You can slide back and sit up.

> *(He turns away and prepares the slide. She gets down and pulls her underwear back on. Once she has finished, she goes to the slide. Conducts the preparation of the slide for the*

microscope. At first they focus themselves on the task...)

NAN. We rinse the slide in different graduated alcohols – 95 percent, 70 percent – then we rehydrate the cells before the hematoxilyn. Then we set the timer.

(They set the timer and wait.)

DR. PAP. What should we talk about?

NAN. Not the fact that I am waiting to know if I have cancer.

DR. PAP. Right.

(A long beat.)

When I was very young my father and I went swimming in the lake outside our town. We swam out to the center, and he told me that I would have to make my own way in the world. They didn't have money, they would help when they could, but I needed to go away and make something of myself. It would not work in Greece.

He told me that if I ever told my mother that he'd said this, he'd deny it. I suppose he knew she'd never forgive him for sending me away. And that's what he was doing. He was sending me away. That was how it felt. Then he swam back to the shore. *(Beat.)* I still dream about him. Every now and then. Sometimes I'm just swimming swimming swimming, but I know he's up ahead somewhere. If I could just catch up.

(The timer dings. They are both very tense.)

NAN. The acid alcohol removes excess hematoxilyn.

Then the tap water substitute, then the OG-6 stain.

(They set the timer. And wait.)

What will you do next?

DR. PAP. Get out of this academic cesspool, open my own research facility, revolutionize women's health. Nothing much.

> *(A beat.)*

NAN. Ted always draws these funny little cartoons.

Odd little cats sitting on a fence with a moon and stars above them.

And he has funny little phrases, like when he gives you a present he always says, "Maybe it's a mechanical mouse!" He says this Every. Time.

Or when we leave for a date he says, "And we're off! – like a herd of blue turtles!"

DR. PAP. *(Trying it out.)* And we're off – like a herd of blue turtles!

That's good. I may keep it.

> *(The timer dings.)*

NAN. A quick rehydration of the cells. And we're ready.

> *(They grow serious. He doesn't want to look at the slide. She doesn't want to look at the slide.)*

DR. PAP. Nan, I don't care what this slide shows me. You should stay. Think of the work you could do, *we* could do.

NAN. Dr. Pap.

DR. PAP. No, listen to me. Just listen:

I want you to listen very carefully.

And don't listen with the regular you,

Tall, true Nan you.

I want you to listen with the *secret* you,

the one that is talking to you even now –

it's there in the background, like a little whisper –

bss bss bss bss bss –

listen from there...

I am going to open this research center. Entirely devoted to women's health.

I am going to need an assistant.

More than an assistant, a partner.

Someone to carry the work forward.

It should be you! It must be you.

Bss bss bss bss bss.

> *(A beat as she listens to her secret self.)*

NAN. I cannot accept.

DR. PAP. Nan! You said you wanted to be a part of something that *lasts*! To leave your mark!

NAN. I don't know if I'll get to have that.

Ted and I are going to make a life together.

I hope I'll have my work, I really do.

I'll have to see how all this *(Meaning her body.)* goes.

But for now.

This is the choice I'm making.

Even my secret self –

bss bss bss bss bss –

tells me this is my choice.

> *(There's nothing else to say.)*

DR. PAP. Very well.

(He looks to the microscope.)

Let's see what we have here.

*(He moves the slide around slowly in the zigzag formation, looking for any abnormal cells. **NAN** thinks about the future she wants with **TED**; little Sara and little Mark. She thinks about her father's toe; hanging the tag on his foot. She thinks about her secret self. After a minute he looks up.)*

Nan. I see nothing.

NAN. Really?

DR. PAP. Absolutely nothing. Your cells are completely normal.

(A beat.)

NAN. I don't know whether to be happy or disappointed.

DR. PAP. Be happy. You don't have cancer.

NAN. But if I don't have cancer, then I have something else.

And I don't know what.

(They sit with that for a moment.)

Can I look?

(She looks down into the microscope at her own cells.)

There I am. That's me.

There's a whole galaxy in there.

(He watches with great affection and sadness. He'll miss her.)

DR. PAP. Yes there is, Nan. Yes there is.

(The light changes, softens into something warmer. **DR. PAP** *addresses the audience.)*

Nan – *Grace* – goes on to Mass General Hospital pathology ward.

It just so happens that Mass General is investigating a new disease called Multiple Sclerosis (MS), and this is how Nan finally uncovers the source of her ailment.

Nan is so good at her job that the hospital sets up a lab *in her home* so she can continue working, even after her MS makes it impossible for her to commute.

So every single day, a wooden crate full of lab samples arrives at the house, and she sits at her microscope at the dining room table and analyzes the slides. She then sends her notes back to the hospital (with the crate), and the next day she receives a new crate with new slides.

Hundreds of crates, with hundreds of slides, analyzing the cancer of hundreds of women.

*(***NAN*** *stands there in the light, and then* ***OLDER NAN*** *[played by* ***MACHE*** *], comes out and stands with her. They are wearing the same thing. They look at one another.)*

Over time, her body changes.

*(***OLDER NAN*** *mirrors what* ***DR. PAP*** *describes.)*

It slows down, wears down, curls down.

Her arms and legs atrophy, so she can only use her left arm.

She and Ted have two children, Sara and Mark.

They're preacher kids. Which is kind of a thing, you know.

But they go on to do good things in the world.

Her daughter Sara marries a teacher.

And so eventually Nan and Ted have *grandchildren*.

Who also go on to do good things in the world.

One becomes a high school principal.

One becomes a preacher, like Ted.

And one becomes a *playwright*.

> (**NAN** *has become* **NAN***'s granddaughter, the playwright. But* **DR. PAP** *doesn't go. From the lab, from the half light, he watches as…*)

Seven

(Fifty years later. **NAN***'s granddaughter,* **THE PLAYWRIGHT***, enters like a small tornado.)*

THE PLAYWRIGHT. Shit guys! –

OLDER TED. Here she comes!

THE PLAYWRIGHT. Sorry I'm late!

OLDER NAN. You're fine.

OLDER TED. Here we are ladies.

(He hands them two glasses of purplish orangish drink.)

THE PLAYWRIGHT. What is this? And don't say it's a mechanical mouse.

OLDER TED. But maybe it is! Maybe it's a mechanical mouse!

OLDER NAN. It's orange juice and cranberry juice.

OLDER TED. It's called Nan's Favorite Drink.

OLDER NAN. Sara named it.

THE PLAYWRIGHT. Okay Grampy get out of here, I wanna talk to Nan.

OLDER TED. About what?

THE PLAYWRIGHT. The vagina.

OLDER TED. Oh hanfry. I'm off, like a herd of blue turtles!

(He's gone.)

THE PLAYWRIGHT. To you, madam.

(They clink glasses.)

OLDER NAN. Ching!

THE PLAYWRIGHT. *(Like a weird pirate.)* Skoal!

(They sip.)

Only Mom would name something Nan's Favorite Drink. This is what your daughter said today, swear to God, I'm not making this up – we're all sitting at the table – you and Gramps were at the church thing – and Mom suddenly says, middle of nowhere –

(À la Sara, whose voice has a dreamy, child-like cadence.)

What *is* a dominatrix?

*(**OLDER NAN**'s laugh is like air sucking through a warm, moist bag.)*

OLDER NAN. Oh Sara!

THE PLAYWRIGHT. *(Laughing too.)* Was she always such a weirdo?

OLDER NAN. Yes.

THE PLAYWRIGHT. *(Laughing.)* Who'd she get that from?

OLDER NAN. *(Duh.)* Ted.

*(**THE PLAYWRIGHT**'s laugh is like two sacks of flesh clapping really loudly.)*

THE PLAYWRIGHT. Ha ha!

OLDER NAN. I remember one time, this was when we lived in Lunenberg, I was working at the table with my lab equipment, and your mom Sara came home...

THE PLAYWRIGHT. Right your lab was at home because of your MS. You must've been *really fucking good* for the hospital to do that.

OLDER NAN. I think it was something like that.

THE PLAYWRIGHT. *(Loving it.)* Haaaa okay go on.

OLDER NAN. So little Sara comes in with her friend and says very proudly, My mother works on cancer of the *Pa-gina. (Said like "vagina" just with a "p".)*

> *(It's like little Sara learned the vagina hazing game Pap used to play!)*

THE PLAYWRIGHT. *(Laughing.)* Oh no.

OLDER NAN. Oh yes. And she's going on, soooo proud, "The *Pa-gina* can get cancer, so the hospital tests your *Pa-gina*, and then *my mother* looks at the tests."

THE PLAYWRIGHT. What's the little friend doing?

OLDER NAN. Trying not to pass out.

THE PLAYWRIGHT. Oh Mom! *(À la Sara.)* "What *is* a dominatrix? And do they have a Pa-gina?"

> *(They enjoy a loving, ruthless laugh at Sara. Maybe* **DR. PAP** *enjoys it too.)*

OLDER NAN. She was always funny. Usually unintentionally.

THE PLAYWRIGHT. So what happened to Dr. Pap?

> *(It's as if* **OLDER NAN** *can sense him, feel him near.)*

OLDER NAN. He did everything he set out to do. He established the Pap smear, opened a research center, revolutionized women's health...well, as you know, because you've been getting a routine Pap smear since...

THE PLAYWRIGHT. *(Not shy or weird about it.)* – Since I started having sex. So – yeah, fifteen.

OLDER NAN. *(Shocked but not offended.)* Fifteen?! Hanfry.

THE PLAYWRIGHT. I'm an overachiever.

OLDER NAN. Ha! *(Beat. Remembering him.)* And then he died. Dr. Pap. 1962. He and Mache moved to Florida to run the Papanicolaou Cancer Research Institute, and he died. Right before it opened. Mache carried on his work without him.

(A beat while that settles.)

THE PLAYWRIGHT. What would have happened? If you'd stayed with Dr. Pap...

OLDER NAN. I bet wonderful things would have happened. And wonderful things would have been lost. Maybe there'd be no Sara. Maybe there'd be no you. That's the thing about life – it's wonderful and sad no matter what.

THE PLAYWRIGHT. *(Struck.)* How do you know? How do you know which wonderful and sad things to choose?

*(That makes **OLDER NAN** laugh her laugh. But then she really thinks on it, still smiling.)*

OLDER NAN. Your secret self.

THE PLAYWRIGHT. Your secret self? What do you mean?

OLDER NAN. You know how we're sitting here, talking, drinking Nan's Favorite Drink...?

Your secret self is behind that, quieter, like pencils on paper, a *bss bss bss* sound.

THE PLAYWRIGHT. *Bss bss bss bss bss.*

OLDER NAN. That's right. She tells you what to do. Even if at the time it involves great loss. She's always right.

*(They both sit with that for a moment. **DR. PAP** exits into the dark. **THE PLAYWRIGHT**'s secret self tells her what she needs to say. What she in fact wrote the play to say.)*

THE PLAYWRIGHT. I'm sorry. I've always wanted to tell you that.

OLDER NAN. Why are you sorry?

THE PLAYWRIGHT. I don't know, for everything.

I'm sorry I didn't write you more.

OLDER NAN. You did write.

THE PLAYWRIGHT. Not enough. There are so many times I could have written.

I'm sorry I didn't – sit like this with you more.

That I didn't ask you more questions about your life.

That we never had this conversation.

That we didn't actually know each other very well.

Like you'll never know my plays.

OLDER NAN. I would love to know your plays.

THE PLAYWRIGHT. I know...

> *(It's as if the space around them is expanding.)*

You're seeing one now. This is one of my plays.

OLDER NAN. *(Gazing out into the dark, an enchanting idea.)* It is?

> *(***THE PLAYWRIGHT** *nods.)*

(Large, still enchanted.) Is it going well?

THE PLAYWRIGHT. *(Equally large, equally enchanted.)* It's hard to tell.

That's the thing about plays.

They go well and don't go well no matter what.

> *(They sit together, looking out. The lights have begun to dim until the light is golden, like a dream.)*

OLDER NAN. How does it end?

THE PLAYWRIGHT. *(Realizing.)* Like this.

Nan and the playwright are together.

Floating in a womb of light.

We look out into this galaxy of stars,

like blinking eyes,

twinkling back at us.

And we're together.

Somehow.

We're together.

> *(They rest like that, floating in the dream. Until blackout.)*

End of Play

www.ingramcontent.com/pod-product-compliance
Lightning Source LLC
Chambersburg PA
CBHW070642120726
47909CB00004B/1538